Put Beginning Readers on the Right Track with
ALL ABOARD READING™

The All Aboard Reading series is especially for beginning readers. Written by noted authors and illustrated in full color, these are books that children really and truly *want* to read—books to excite their imagination, tickle their funny bone, expand their interests, and support their feelings. With three different reading levels, All Aboard Reading lets you choose which books are most appropriate for your children and their growing abilities.

Level 1—for Preschool through First Grade Children
Level 1 books have very few lines per page, very large type, easy words, lots of repetition, and pictures with visual "cues" to help children figure out the words on the page.

Level 2—for First Grade to Third Grade Children
Level 2 books are printed in slightly smaller type than Level 1 books. The stories are more complex, but there is still lots of repetition in the text and many pictures. The sentences are quite simple and are broken up into short lines to make reading easier.

Level 3—for Second Grade through Third Grade Children
Level 3 books have considerably longer texts, use harder words and more complicated sentences.

All Aboard for happy reading!

Developed by The Philip Lief Group, Inc.

Copyright © 1986 by The Philip Lief Group, Inc. New material copyright © 1994 by Grosset & Dunlap, Inc. Based upon the series KITTEN KIDS™ by Tomie dePaola, published by Little Simon, a division of Simon & Schuster, Inc. All rights reserved. Published by Grosset & Dunlap, Inc., a member of The Putnam & Grosset Group, New York. GROSSET & DUNLAP is a trademark of Grosset & Dunlap, Inc. ALL ABOARD READING is a trademark of The Putnam & Grosset Group. KITTEN KIDS is a trademark of The Philip Lief Group, Inc. Published simultaneously in Canada. Printed in the U.S.A.

Library of Congress Cataloging-in-Publication Data

dePaola, Tomie.
    Kit and Kat / by Tomie dePaola.
       p.   cm. — (All aboard reading)
    Summary: Three stories featuring the Kitten Kids sleeping at their grandparents' house, riding bikes, and playing with a bully.
    1. Children's stories, American. [1. Brothers and sisters—Fiction.   2. Cats—Fiction.]
I. Title.   II. Series.
PZ7.D439Kav   1994
[E]—dc20   94-15070
                                                                                     CIP
ISBN 0-448-40749-3 (GB)   A B C D E F G H I J   AC

ISBN 0-448-40748-5 (pbk.)   A B C D E F G H I J

ALL
ABOARD
READING™

Level 1
Preschool-Grade 1

KIT and KAT

Written and illustrated by
Tomie dePaola

Grosset & Dunlap • New York

Kit's Pajamas

Today was a big day
for Kit and Kat.

They were going to sleep at
Grandma and Grandpa's house.

Kit and Kat got out their stuff.

Soon they were ready.

"Do you have everything?"
asked Grandma.

"Yes," said Kit.

"Yes," said Kat.

So off they went.

Kit and Kat had fun.

Grandpa gave the best rides.

Grandma read the best stories.

Soon it was time for bed.

Kat put on her pajamas.

But Kit could not find his.

"I left them at home!"
said Kit.
And he began to cry.

"Don't cry," said Grandpa.

"Look!"

"Oh, Grandpa," said Kit.

"Your pajama top!"

"You look like
a little Grandpa,"
said Kat.

Then they both went to sleep.

Kat's Good Idea

One day, Kit and Kat
got a big surprise
from Mom and Dad.

Two bikes!

Kat got a red bike.

Kit got a blue bike.

"Let's race!"

said Kat.

She got on the red bike.

Off she went.

"I WIN!"

said Kat.

Kit got on the blue bike.

But he did not move.

"I am too little," he said.

"My feet do not reach

the pedals."

Kat had an idea.
She got two blocks.

Kat put the blocks
on the pedals.

"Your feet will reach now,"
said Kat.
Then Kit got on his bike.
His feet <u>did</u> reach!

Off he went.
"I WIN!" said Kit
to Kat.

Kit, Kat, and the Bully

Kit and Kat were having fun.

They were playing with blocks.

Then Tom came over.

Tom was no fun.

What did Tom do?

He kicked the blocks.

"Blocks are for babies,"
said Tom.

Then Tom said,
"Let's go on the seesaw.
The seesaw is fun."

But the seesaw
was no fun—

not with Tom.

"Now I want to ride
in your car," said Tom.
"But you are too big,"
said Kat.
"No, I'm not!"
said Tom.

Tom got in.

He <u>was</u> too big.

He got stuck.

"Help!" cried Tom.

"Help! Help!"

"Say the magic word," said Kat.

"Please," said Tom.

But that was not enough.

"Pretty please," said Tom.

But that was not enough.

"Pretty please with sugar
on top," said Tom.
<u>That</u> was enough.
Kit and Kat pulled Tom
out of the car.

And Tom did not
act like a bully—
for the rest of that day!